Anna Joujan
ADMIRER

Gordie Hayduk
ARTIST

MY OWN FLOWER PICTURE

Kimon Scott Iannetta
DAUGHTER

Amy Ehrlich
EDITOR

Sue Adabody
SISTER

Caroline Alexandra Foti
GREAT-GRANDDAUGHTER

Kathy Vail
FRIEND

Tom Layou
FRIEND

Yolanda LeRoy
EDITOR

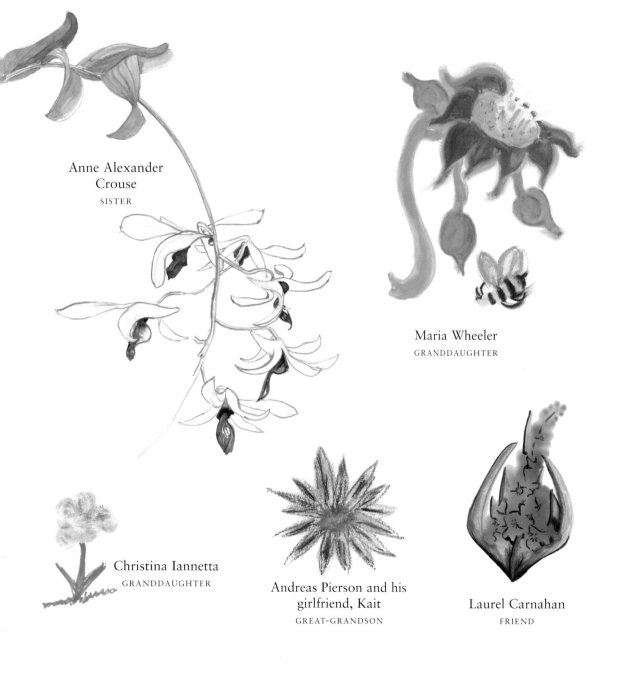

Anne Alexander
Crouse
SISTER

Maria Wheeler
GRANDDAUGHTER

Christina Iannetta
GRANDDAUGHTER

Andreas Pierson and his
girlfriend, Kait
GREAT-GRANDSON

Laurel Carnahan
FRIEND

# Max and the Dumb Flower Picture

## MARTHA ALEXANDER

*with James Rumford*

ini Charlesbridge

# In Memory of Martha Alexander
## 1920-2006

Text copyright © 2009 by the Estate of Martha Alexander
Illustrations copyright © 2009 by the Estate of Martha Alexander with James Rumford
All rights reserved, including the right of reproduction in whole or in part in any form.
Charlesbridge and colophon are registered trademarks of Charlesbridge Publishing, Inc.

Published by Charlesbridge
85 Main Street
Watertown, MA 02472
(617) 926-0329
www.charlesbridge.com

**Library of Congress Cataloging-in-Publication Data**
Alexander, Martha G.
    Max and the dumb flower picture / Martha Alexander; illustrated by Martha
Alexander and James Rumford.
        p. cm.
    Summary: Despite his teacher's entreaties that it would be perfect for Mother's Day,
Max refuses to color in the same flower picture as the rest of the class.
    ISBN 978-1-58089-156-1 (reinforced for library use)
[1. Individuality—Fiction. 2. Teachers—Fiction. 3. Mother's Day—Fiction.]
I. Rumford, James, 1948– ill. II. Title.
PZ7.A3777Max 2009
[E]—dc22         2008007251

Printed in China
(hc) 10 9 8 7 6 5 4 3 2 1

Sketches were drawn by Martha Alexander and James Rumford, manipulated and
    partially colored digitally, then printed on drawing paper and watercolored by hand.
Display type set in Mrs. Eaves, designed by Zuzana Lickle for Emigre
Text type set in Sabon
Color separations by Chroma Graphics, Singapore
Printed and bound by Regent Publishing Services
Production supervision by Brian G. Walker
Designed by Susan Mallory Sherman

Max didn't want to color the dumb flower picture. Miss Tilley wanted him to.

"Your mother will love it," she said.

Max knew his mother wouldn't love it.

Sunday was Mother's Day, though, and he needed a present.

Miss Tilley made copies of the dumb
flower picture for everyone to color.
She kept saying, "Make the flowers pretty."

Max didn't want to color in the lines of the dumb flower picture. Miss Tilley wanted him to.

"You'll be the only one without a nice picture for your mother," she said.

Max knew his mother didn't like coloring books, and he knew she wouldn't like a dumb flower picture, either.

He knew she would rather have his very
own drawing.

Max just sat there and sat there.

The other children did what Miss Tilley wanted them to do. They stayed in the lines and made the flowers pretty.

Not Max.

Max stomped his feet and sulked.

Max couldn't sit there any longer.

The other children went looking for him.
Miss Tilley was worried that he had
run away.

She called the police to help look for him.

After a while Abbey called, "Here he is!
I found him!" Max came out from behind
the bushes.

The policeman was glad to see that Max
was safe.

Miss Tilley was glad that Max hadn't
run away.

Max hid his drawing behind his back.
All the children wanted to see it.

Max showed them.

ere happy and excited
resents that their

The children ran back to the classroom.
They got right to work.

Yolanda held up her flower picture.

All five mothers w
about the beautiful p
children had made.

"Each is so different!" they exclaimed.

## A Note from James Rumford

Martha Alexander was a quiet genius. During her long career she used her gentle magic to capture childhood on paper for all to see.

I came to know Martha in her eighties. Before she passed away, we talked a lot about this book and how much it meant to her. She believed that children need to feel the freedom of creativity—to look upon a blank sheet of paper and see possibilities, not limitations brought on by the fear of "not getting it right."

Martha left me with her manuscript and unfinished sketches. Like blank sheets, these sketches had limitless possibilities. So I worked with them, fleshing them out with characters she had created in her other books and with those from her unpublished drawings. With the help of a computer, I let Martha finish her book and work her magic once more.

Jack Prelutsky
POET

Susan Sherman
ART DIRECTOR AND
BOOK DESIGNER

Susan Yelliott
Batten
NIECE

Noah Foti
GREAT-GRANDSON

Sue Cowing
AUTHOR AND POET

David Ford
PUBLISHER

Jane Yelliott
SISTER

Dawson Zimmermann
FRIEND

Leslie Iannetta
GRANDDAUGHTER

Ginnie Hofmann
OLDEST AND DEAREST
FRIEND

Jane and Arnie Westfall
FRIENDS

Lynne Wikoff
AUTHOR